Princess Truly

in My Magical,
SPARKLING CURLS

For Bub, Bug, Kitty, Moo, Roo, and Bunny.
I love you from the tops of your heads to the tips of your toes.

— K.G.

For Junie and Jalen.
You will do extraordinary things!

— A.R.

10 9 8 7 6 5 4 3 2 1   18 19 20 21 22 • Printed in the U.S.A. 40 • First printing 2018 • Book design by Patti Ann Harris

Princess Truly

in My Magical,
SPARKLING CURLS

by
Kelly Greenawalt

illustrated by
Amariah Rauscher

Scholastic Inc.

I love my fluffy, puffy curls.
I'm so happy they are mine.
When I believe in myself,
They shimmer and they shine.

I am bright and I am brilliant.
I can do extraordinary things.
When my hair sparkles and glows,
I can soar without wings.

I wonder what I'll do today.
There is so much to explore.

A little bit of magic,
And I'm on a dinosaur!

We play hopscotch
And hide-and-seek,
And then we have a race.

The giganotosaurus is very fast,
But the T. rex wins first place.

Next, I explore the pyramids
And discover ancient halls.
I find secret messages
Written on the walls.

I am smart and I am clever.
I can crack the code.
I uncover mysteries
Written long ago.

I say goodbye, and off I fly,
Down to the sandy shore.
I climb into a submarine,
And set off to explore.

Happy clams, an octopus,
And lots of colorful fish —
I sure would like to play with them,
And so I make a wish.

I swim around exploring
Along the ocean floor.
I discover new sea creatures
No one's ever seen before.

Then my fluffy, puffy curls
Begin to shine so bright.
I hop into my rocket ship
And zoom into the night.

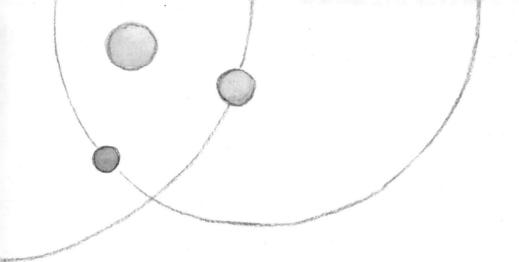

I fly across the galaxy.
I make a map with all the stars.

I count the rings on Jupiter,
Then chart a course to Mars.

I want to hear some music,
And so I start a band.
Just a touch of magic,
And we begin to jam.

We rock 'n' roll and draw a crowd.
Our fans are cheering very loud.

When the show is over,
I wish that I could stay.
But I'm feeling very sleepy.
My curls will light the way.

I love my fluffy, puffy hair.
It is Truly divine.
When I believe in myself,
It shimmers and it shines!

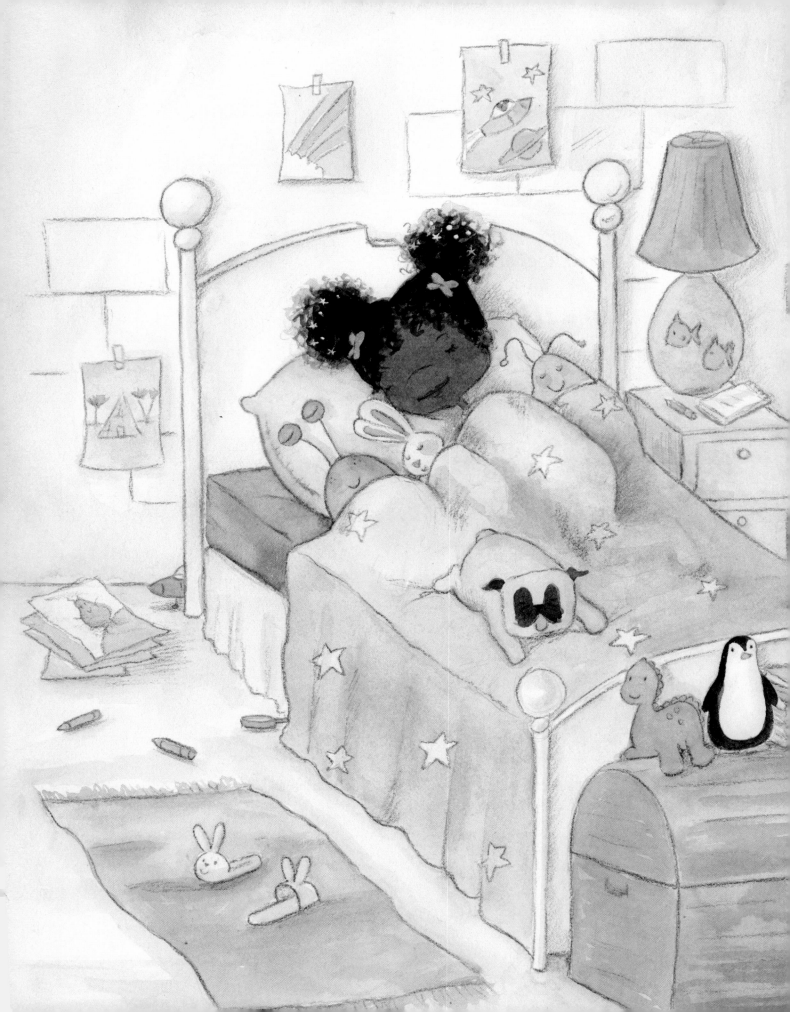

Dear Readers:

We created Princess Truly for our daughters. We wanted them to see a strong, smart, problem-solving, confident young girl with beautiful curls who could do anything she set her mind to! We hope this book inspires readers everywhere to reach for the stars, dream big, and stay TRUE to who they are.

Kelly   *Amariah*

Kelly and her daughters,
Calista and Kaia

Amariah with her daughters,
Jalen and Junie